MR.DIZZY

by Roger Hargreaves

D0109340

© 1976 Roger Hargreaves
Published by Thurman Publishing Ltd.,
The Mill Trading Estate, Acton Lane, London NW10

Mr Dizzy was, to be quite honest, not very clever.

If you were to ask Mr Dizzy what was the opposite of black, he'd say "Er. The opposite of black is . . . er . . . pink!"

He lived in a house on a hill which he'd built himself.

A not very clever house!

One of Mr Dizzy's problems was that he lived in a country where everybody else was terribly clever.

Cleverland!

Even the birds were clever in Cleverland!

Everything and everybody in Cleverland was clever.

You'll never see a worm reading a book anywhere else but Cleverland.

Poor Mr Dizzy. Everything around him was so clever it made his head spin.

One morning Mr Dizzy was out for a walk when he met a pig.

''What's big and grey and has big ears and a trunk?'' said the clever pig to Mr Dizzy.

''Er! A mouse?'' said Mr Dizzy.

The pig laughed sarcastically at Mr Dizzy, and went off shaking his head.

Then Mr Dizzy met an elephant.

A clever elephant.

"What's small and furry and likes cheese?" the elephant asked cleverly.

"Er. A pig?" replied Mr Dizzy.

The clever elephant laughed down his trunk. "A pig?" he trumpeted "A pig? You silly man!" And off he went.

Poor Mr Dizzy!

Mr Dizzy decided he didn't want to talk to anybody else that day, so he went for a walk in the wood, where he knew that he wouldn't meet anybody.

He felt very miserable about not being clever, and as he walked along a tear trickled down his cheek.

Poor Mr Dizzy.

Then, in the middle of the wood, he came across a well.

Little did Mr Dizzy know that it was a wishing well.

The day was warm, and so he decided to take a drink of water from the well.

Mr Dizzy drank deeply.

But, he was still unhappy.

''Oh, I wish I could be clever'' he sighed.

Little did Mr Dizzy know that whoever drinks deeply from the water at the wishing well, his wish will come true.

And Mr Dizzy had wished that he could be clever.

And his wish had come true.

He was clever.

But he didn't know it.

Not yet!

On the way home Mr Dizzy came across the elephant and the pig who he had met earlier.

They were telling each other about how they had made Mr Dizzy look silly by asking him a question he couldn't answer.

They were giggling and sniggering about it when they saw Mr Dizzy approaching from the wood.

''Here he comes again'' giggled the clever pig.

''Let's ask him another question'' sniggered the clever elephant.

Mr Dizzy came up to them.

''Tell us'' said the clever pig, trying to keep a straight face ''What's white and woolly and goes Baaa?''

''Why a sheep of course'' replied Mr Dizzy.

The pig and the elephant were amazed.

To tell the truth, so too was Mr Dizzy.

He suddenly felt very very clever.

It was a not unpleasant feeling.

"Tell us" said the clever elephant "What has four legs, a tail and goes Woof?"

"How easy" replied Mr Dizzy "A dog of course!"

The clever pig and the clever elephant couldn't understand how Mr Dizzy had become so clever in one morning.

Mr Dizzy couldn't understand how he had become so clever in one morning.

But we know how he'd become so clever in one morning.

Don't we?

"Now, let me ask you a question" said Mr Dizzy to the pig.

"You?" grunted the pig rudely "You ask me a question? Don't be ridiculous! There's no question you could ask me that I couldn't answer!"

"Really?" smiled Mr Dizzy "Well then, can you tell me what's fat and pink and goes Atishoo Atishoo?"

"What's fat and pink and goes Atishoo Atishoo?" repeated the pig looking worried "There's nothing that's fat and pink and goes Atishoo Atishoo!"

"Nothing eh?" said Mr Dizzy, and he tickled the pig's nose.

"Atishoo Atishoo" sneezed the pig.

. "The answer is you" said Mr Dizzy "You're fat and pink and you're going Atishoo Atishoo!"

The clever pig looked downright, if not downleft, miserable.

Mr Dizzy turned to the elephant.

Who, incidentally, had stopped sniggering.

"Now" said Mr Dizzy "Let me ask you a question. What's large and grey and goes Dopit Dopit?"

"What's large and grey and goes Dopit Dopit?" repeated the elephant looking worried "There's nothing that's large and grey and goes Dopit Dopit."

"Oh yes there is" grinned Mr Dizzy "There certainly is something that's large and grey and goes Dopit Dopit" and he tied a knot in the clever elephant's trunk.

"Dop it! Dop it!" cried the elephant, who wanted to say "Stop it! Stop it!" But couldn't talk properly with a knot in his trunk.

Mr Dizzy grinned, and went home.

"I duppose doo dink dat's fuddy" said the
elephant.